A Boy Named Neville

by Linda Gambrill

A Beenybud Story

with illustrations by
Marlene Lewis

Published in Jamaica by
Ian Randle Publishers
11 Cunningham Avenue, Kingston 6, Jamaica West Indies
in association with
Premiere Productions Limited

©Linda Gambrill, 1990, 1998, 2008
Illustrations ©Marlene Lewis-Weinberger
Beenybud®

Book and cover design by Marlene Lewis-Weinberger
and Mark Weinberger
Text illustrations by Marlene Lewis-Weinberger

National Library of Jamaica Cataloguing-in-Publication Data

Gambrill, Linda
A Boy Named Neville: a Beenybud story (Beenybud series)

1. Fiction
I. Lewis-Weinberger, Marlene II. Title III. Series
813'.5'4
ISBN 978-976-637-379-5

First published in Jamaica, 1990,
by Heinemann Publishers (Caribbean) Limited

*to Miss Olive and Miss Pearl
who helped in so many ways*

A Beenybud Story

Beenybud and her family are Jamaican. They live in a closeknit, scenically beautiful, rural village, nestled in the Blue Mountains. The capital city, Kingston, lies on the plains below.

Each of these stories tells of Beenybud's experiences. And it is as if she invited you, as a best friend, to read her secret diary, to share these special moments of her life. The writing is, therefore, in Beenybud's own personal style.

My thanks to my husband, Tony, my children, Ashley and Laura, whose love has been my inspiration and my friend and illustrator, Marlene Lewis.

I hope you will become a good friend of Beenybud, and as her grandmother always says, "Walk good!"

Linda Gambrill

My proper name is Elizabeth Angelica Campbell, but everybody calls me Beenybud.

Do you like boys? I do not like them at all, at all! I do not like lizards, and when those boys, including my brother Danny, start chasing us girls around with a lizard dangling from a coconut loop... I get very, very angry. There was a boy in our village named Neville Robinson, he was the worst! He was so facety! He had no manners.

He and his grandmother, Miss Mary, came to live in Merryfield Village some while ago. They lived up at Fernfield Road in a house with a whole heap of mauger dogs that were very cross.

Miss Mary was always sickly. She stayed in her

house all the time. So nobody much ever visited them.

Neville is, I feel, about twelve years old, because he is much taller than me and I am nearly ten years old. Still, he was in my class at St. Mathew's Primary, and I knew I could read and write much better than him.

But that was because he hardly ever came to school. And when he came, he always came late and most of the time he was not very tidy.

Teacher, Mrs. Clarke, used to get very angry with him, but he did not seem to care. She always used to tell him, "Neville Robinson, you have no ambition!"

But, as I see it, Neville had ambition but did not feel

he had to go to any school. He
was always boasting that when
we did not see him in the village,
he had gone down to Kingston to
help his uncle who had one big-
time haberdashery by Parade.

Then again, he told us that his father lived in England
and had bags of money, and when he, Neville, got to be
a big man, his father was going to send for him to work
in his business.

Well, my mama said to my brother, "Is that so? God
bless the child that has his own. And you, Mr. Daniel

Campbell, better form no fool. Mind how you keep company with that worthless boy because you, sir, are staying right here in Jamaica!"

Neville told us his father sent him and his granny money every month. Also, Neville made his own money. He built himself a pushcart, which he ran up and down Fernfield Road. He charged one dollar a turn if you wanted a ride, fifty cents if you pushed the cart back up the hillside.

I was always frightened to go on it, and besides, there was a lawyer lady that lived on the road and went to my mama's church. Every afternoon when the business was in full swing, she would rush out of her house like she was mad.

"Neville Robinson, this has got to stop! It's dangerous! I am going to tell Miss Mary. You should not be doing this. Suppose a car comes up the road while these poor children are going down? I am tired of telling you the same thing every afternoon, and besides, it's baby's rest time. I cannot stand the noise!"

Neville was provoking for true! Like the time I was walking home with some things from the shop for Mama. I was minding my own business when I spotted Neville dilly-dallying down the road.

Next thing he called out, "Hi there, Beeny Baby!"

"If you call me that again, Neville Robinson, I going tell my mama!"

He made one monkey face after me. "Eh-hee now! Cry-cry baby, moonshine darling! Beeny Baby, Beeny Baby! Mama's little baby!" he bawled out in a loud sing-song you could hear clear down the village.

I cut my eye after him. "Well at least I have a mama, Neville Robinson."

I was so vexed! Neville gave me a hard look. The sun beat down on the top of my head. The old mash-up asphalt road looked like it was melting; it was burning my foot-bottom through my crepe shoes.

All of a sudden Neville took something out of his pocket and pushed it in front of my face.

"You want to see something, Elizabeth Angelica Campbell? You think you live in any big, fancy house! Look at this picture my father just sent me of where he lives!"

I barely looked at the shaking picture, but it was really a big house for true, favour any palace. "So what, Neville Robinson! Look 'pon you foot, favour two drumstick!"

He gave out a big laugh. "Koo you, petchary!"

The next day at school, Mrs. Clarke gave us a very interesting lesson, all about England. I had taken a big soursop in my bag to give Neville for his granny, as Mama says it is good for the nerves.

Neville never came to school that day. So I decided on my way home to stop off at Neville's house.

When I reached Neville's gate, all the mauger dogs rushed out same time and started one big barking. I frighten of dog like any puss.

"Neville, Neville!" I bawled out.

"Who that?" Miss Mary came out of the house.

"Is me, Ma'am, Miss Beulah's daughter, Beenybud. Howdy-do. I'm looking for Neville, Miss Mary."

"Neville? Me not feeling so copacetic today, child. Pupalopse, stop the barking! Lord them dog just barking barking in my ears! Don't today is Thursday? Every Thursday, rain or shine, from before day Neville gone down to Coronation Market to sell the little provisions from the field. Him no reach back till Sunday morning. God bless the child! Any message, my love?"

"No, Ma'am, is all right. I hope you feel better soon soon. Oh, my mama send you this pretty soursop for your nerves."

"Thank you, my child. Who you say? Miss Beulah daughter? Oh yes, the nice family that live 'cross the river. Neville tell me 'bout you all the time. The Lord willing me will feel better. God bless you, my love."

Monday morning, Neville turned up at school. Casual like, I said to him, "Neville, we missed you over the weekend. You were helping your uncle at the haberdashery?"

"Beenybud, why you so small and so interfering? Yes, I was with my uncle. Cho, you think your Miss Milly has a shop? Cho, you should see my uncle's shop! 'La Emporium'! Full of things from America! One fancy store, you see, man! On Parade."

"Neville, you missed an interesting lesson on Thursday. All about England, where your father lives. I went by your house to tell you all about it, but you were not there."

"What my grandmother tell you? She not sort of all there, you know."

"She didn't say anything strange. She was not feeling too well. I gave her a soursop my mama sent for her. Neville, you know the house you said was your father's house? It is called Buckingham Palace. The Queen of England lives there too!"

"Then don't I tell you that my father has money, man! You tell teacher or anybody else?"

"No, I never had any cause to tell her, Neville, and I figure you would not want any and everybody to know your father is so stoshus! It is our secret, but I want you to try and behave yourself better and try to be nicer to Mrs. Clarke."

Neville looked at me in a very strange way, like he wanted to say something. "Petchary," he started to say. But then the bell rang and I hurried to get into the line. I could still feel his eyes hard on my back.

I made up my mind, standing in the line—it was so hot all of a sudden—that I was not going to tell anybody the secrets I had learnt about Neville. I do not know why, but I was going to give him a chance. I felt for certain there were a lot of other things he was hiding from us. And then, that very Sunday evening, something happened that I knew in my heart, I would never, never ever forget.

We were having dinner when we heard a loud knocking at the front door. Mama went to see who it was. It was Miss Mary. "You see Neville anywhere, Miss Beulah?"

"No, Miss Mary. I do not know the day last I've seen Neville. Please, come inside, Ma'am. Beeny, Danny, you know where Neville is?"

Before we could say a

word, Miss Mary crumpled down at the doorstep. We all rushed to see what had happened.

Mama and Papa knelt down beside her. "Miss Mary, Miss Mary!" they called out, but Miss Mary never said a word.

"Lord my God! Ralph, you think she is dead?" Mama cried.

"No. Come, Danny, help me to lift her into the bedroom." Papa carried her gently, like a baby, in his arms, till he laid her down on the bed.

Danny was sent quickly to call Dr. Smith and to look for Neville. Meanwhile, we stayed by Miss Mary's bedside. I started to cry, for poor Miss Mary looked so old, just lying down so still in the bed.

All of a sudden she opened her eyes and started to whisper something, so softly you could hardly hear her. "Neville...Neville...me want Neville..." That was all she said. She looked hard up at the ceiling and her eyes filled with water.

"Neville soon soon come, Miss Mary. Do, no distress yourself," my mama begged, as she cradled Miss Mary's hand and softly patted it.

We all looked at each other and then towards the door, but there was no sign of Neville.

Miss Mary's eyes closed again and a smile crossed her mouth like she was dreaming a sweet dream.

Mama sent me to go look down the end of the garden to see if I see the doctor or Neville coming, while she went into the kitchen to make some green tea for Miss Mary.

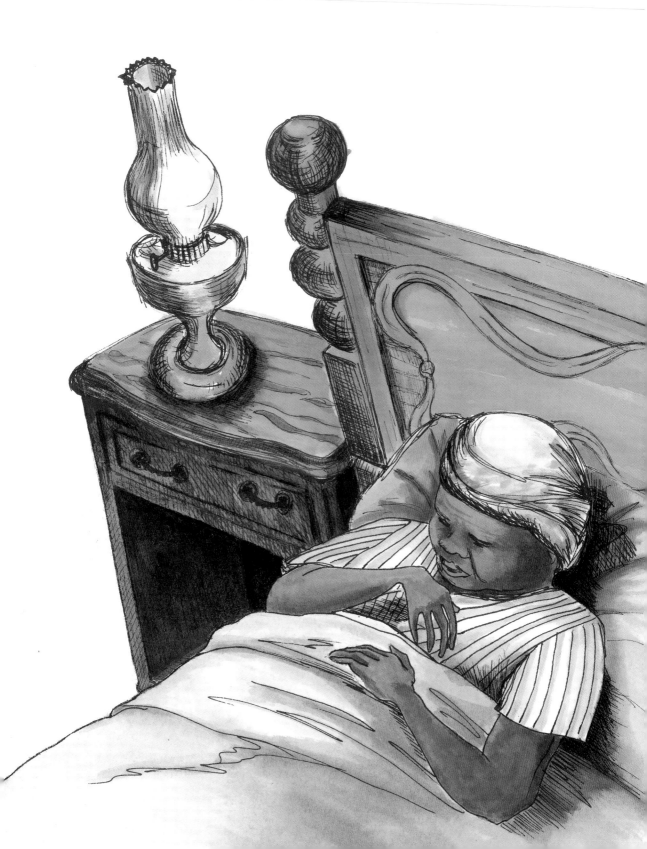

It was a beautiful moonshine night. I took Maria, my pet goat, down the road with me, but not a living soul was to be seen. I looked up at the big everlasting yellow moon.

Everything shone in its bright light, the banana leaves like silver ribbons, the mountains like guardian angels glowing, with their wings spread wide against the night, all around me, watching. The night-blooming jasmine smelt so sweet.

Maria rubbed her cold nose on my bare leg. It was so peaceful, like an

old church. A choir of whistling frogs and the splattering of the river alone broke the stillness of the sweet night air.

I knelt down on the cold wet grass. "Sweet Jesus, I beg you, help Miss Mary. Just let Neville come."

When I got back into Miss Mary's room I heard her saying to Mama, "Miss Beulah, me have to talk. My time come. I am not afraid, for I am ready to meet my Maker. Me only want to see Neville now...to hold him hand. Miss Beulah, do, sing me a hymn, a sweet, pretty song."

She turned her head towards the wall but you could still see she was crying.

"When me think how since we come to this village and me get old and sickly, him look after me. 'Stead of going to school, him stay home many a day, cook my food, wash my clothes, even plant vegetable in the yard and sell it in the market, just to get some money for we to live. By the grace of God we manage, and Neville save me from the fear that we would turn beggar."

"Him never did ask anyone to help. Him do it all with a steadfast heart."

Mama turned to Papa and whispered, "Lord, Ralph, what happen to the doctor and Neville? I feel she is going to die. They say these old-time people know when their time comes, you know.

You think is the truth she is talking? But don't the children tell me that Neville's father in England is supposed to send them money every month?"

Miss Mary shook her head, "Me 'member everything like it was yesterday. Neville, you nearly a big man now. But you come to me a few months old, wrap up in one towel. You mother, poor soul, dead and gone. You father, him so wort'less, nobody even know where him is...is me one raise you!"

She could barely speak. Then she suddenly lifted herself up off the pillow and tightly squeezed Mama's hand.

"Miss Beulah, Miss Beulah...me have some money, not much, under my bed, wrap up in one red cloth for the day of tomorrow...tell Neville say me save it for him education...it not too late...me want him to go to school and turn big man...like what him dream 'bout."

Just then Neville ran into the room. "I come, Mama...I come..."

Papa took our hands and led us out of the room.

Miss Mary died that night. Neville told Mama she just squeezed his hands and fell asleep with a smile on her face...peaceful...peaceful.

Mama and Papa decided that Neville should stay with us a while. You never saw anyone changed so! Neville became quiet. It was the hardest thing to get him to talk. I could tell he was sad, but from the night Miss Mary died he never let anyone see him cry.

When Papa told Neville about the money, and what Miss Mary wanted it for, he said, "Mr. Ralph, it is my money now. My grandmother saved it but I worked hard for it. I will manage for myself. My grandmother was a good and decent lady. I do not want people to say her family never cared for her. It is not her fault. No, sir, I am going to use that money and give her a good funeral! One she can be proud of!"

So Papa and Mama helped Neville with all the arrangements. We had a nice set-up for her at our house, and Mr. Augustus St. Alban was in charge of the singing.

And Neville did what he set out to do. He gave Miss Mary a beautiful funeral. Everybody in the village turned out. Althea, my big sister, sang 'Amazing Grace' and the people cried and cried.

Neville, with his old boasty ways, even put an announcement in the Gleaner about Miss Mary's death, which, as my mama said, was an Angel of God at work. A few days later, a foreign gentleman arrived at our home. He drove up our drive-way in one brand new motor car, and introduced himself to us as Mr. Horatio Robinson of Newark, New Jersey.

"Neville, I am your Uncle Horatio! Miss Mary's eldest son!" the gentleman said. "I have been residing in America for the past forty years. Just yesterday, I return home for the first time. It was my dearest intention to find my mother and try to make up to her for all those lost, forgotten years. Instead, imagine my shock and sadness on being greeted by the news of her death. I saw your notice that appeared in the local newspaper. I was too late."

"My wife and I have no children of our own. We have recently retired and we are planning to purchase a property in Clarendon, and to live there. Neville, please, I would like you to come and live with us and be our son."

A big commotion broke out in the house same time! There was much talking and even crying, and everyone was so happy for Neville, for as my mama said, he certainly deserved it!

Although I was happy for Neville's sake, I do not
know why, but the day he was to leave us, I felt sad.
I had wanted for a long time to talk to him, to tell
him the things that were in my heart. But everytime
I got a chance, my mouth turned funny and I never
knew what to say.

Neville was packing his things. Mama had given me the clothes she had ironed for him.

Standing there, alone with him in the room, the neatly folded clothes across my arms, before I knew what, I said, "Neville, I feel like you are going to be happy now."

He took the clothes I gave him, and smiled. "I feel so, Beeny. The only thing is...I going to miss all of you

and this house. You are like the only real family I ever lived with...is hard to explain..."

And he stopped and started packing his few things. I was not sure if he had finished what he wanted to say. I felt very peculiar. I did not know what to say or do.

"You see..." he continued, "you see, Miss Mary and me, we were different. Ever since I can remember, I looked after her and minded her.

We had good times together, she and me...she was always full of jokes...I miss her..." He had finished packing his little suitcase.

"Papa said he will take us to visit you, and Mr. Horatio said that he will bring you to visit us too!"

I felt my mouth going funny again, like when you have just eaten a sour, stainy guinep. I swallowed hard. I felt for sure I was going to cry! But quickly I said—I do not know why I said it—"Promise me, promise me, you not going to turn big shot, now that you really have money. And promise me you are going to go to school and study your lessons hard. And that you are not going to get into any fights, because, Neville, I like you just the way you are now!"

Neville smiled. "Petchary...you sound just like my grandmother!"

I saw his eyes were full of water and I could feel it welling up in mine...so, I quickly left the room.

GLOSSARY

Copacetic	very good.
Dilly-dally	procrastinating.
Facety	rude, impertinent.
Favour	to look like.
Fret	grieve, worry.
Guinep	a fruit popular with children.
Mauger	thin, underfed.
Petchary	small bird.
Soursop	a fruit usually made into juice.
Stoshus	high class.
Vex	angry.
Walk good	safe journey, keep well on your way.

...and as my grandmother always says,
"Walk good"